To all the parents struggling to protect their children and elevate their souls—with love
—L.S.

To my three "little" sisters, Donna, Dana, and Dawn, who still continue to humble, amaze, and inspire me
—D.M.

Growing Up Is Hard
Text copyright © 2001 by Dr. Laura Schlessinger
Illustrations copyright © 2001 by Daniel McFeeley
Printed in the United States. All rights reserved.
www.harperchildrens.com

Library of Congress Cataloging-in-Publication Data
Schlessinger, Laura.
    Growing up is hard / by Laura Schlessinger ; illustrated by Daniel McFeeley. — 1st ed.
       p.   cm.
    Summary: When a young boy has a day where nothing goes right, his father helps him deal with his feelings and see that things change as he grows up.
    ISBN 0-06-029200-8. — ISBN 0-06-029201-6 (lib. bdg.)
    [1. Fathers and sons—Fiction. 2. Growth—Fiction.] I. McFeeley, Dan, ill. II. Title.
PZ7.S347115 Ih 2001   00-33578
[E]—dc21   CIP

1 2 3 4 5 6 7 8 9 10

First Edition

Dr. Laura Schlessinger's
Growing up Is Hard

Illustrated by Daniel McFeeley

Cliff Street Books
An Imprint of HarperCollinsPublishers

Sammy sat on the front stoop, his shoulders hunched over as he held his face in both hands.

"Sammy," said Dad as he walked up the front walkway from his car, "you look so sad. What's wrong? Has something happened?"

"Nothing, Daddy," answered Sammy without raising his head. "Nothing," he repeated even more softly.

"Sammy, let's go for a walk together," offered Dad.

"I don't want to. I don't really feel like it." Sammy got up to walk into the house.

Dad followed Sammy into the kitchen. He asked again, "Sammy, please, honey, tell me what's wrong."

Just then Sammy accidentally dropped the milk carton. He screamed, *"Nothing is wrong! Everything is wrong! I just hate my life!"*

Sammy ran out of the house crying and yelling over and over, *"I hate my life!"* Dad followed close behind.

When Dad caught up with Sammy, he picked him up in his big strong daddy arms and held him tight. All the while, Sammy wiggled and wriggled and yelled. Finally, Sammy collapsed in his dad's arms and cried and cried.

After Sammy had cried out all his tears, Dad told him, "Sammy, Mommy and I love you very much. We are both here to help you when your body hurts, when your heart hurts, and when your thoughts hurt. Sometimes it's hard to talk about the hurts in your heart or thoughts, but that's the best way to make things better and to feel better."

Sammy said, "But Daddy, there are a bunch of things making me feel bad. If I tell you some of the things you might think I'm stupid or bad. Then I'll feel worse."

Dad thought about what Sammy said. "Sammy, I know what you're saying. Sometimes I feel the same way. When I have troubles or problems and want to talk them over with your mother, sometimes I worry that she'll think I'm stupid or bad."

"Really?" said Sammy, surprised.

"Really," said Dad. "But after I get the words out, my problems don't really seem so bad. And Mommy is always understanding and helpful. Even though sometimes I'm scared to tell her everything in my mind and heart, I trust her love and it all works out."

"Yeah. Okay." Sammy took a deep breath. "Well, things are just so different than they used to be," he began.

"What do you mean?" asked Dad.

"Whenever I used to draw a picture, you and Mommy and Grandma and Gramps always made a big deal. You said how wonderful it was and gave me hugs and kisses. Yesterday in kindergarten, Miss Caroline told me my picture could be better. I felt really bad. And then I was angry at her.

"And when I asked Peter at lunch if he could come over and play after school today, he said he couldn't because he was going to play with Kenny. I got mad because Peter's *my* friend!

"And when I got home," continued Sammy, getting out of breath, "Mommy said that she already told me two times that I was supposed to take the trash bags out. Because I forgot she said I couldn't watch my favorite TV show tonight.

"And the other day Grandma yelled at me because I was painting my desk chair purple with the spray can and got it on the floor. She said I was acting like a baby. She said I was big enough to know better.

"I don't want to be big enough. Everything used to be . . . everything used to be . . . nicer. Now everything is different." Sammy started to cry again.

"Oh," said Dad, putting his arm around Sammy. They walked over to a tree in the park and sat down. "I think I understand what the problem is.

"Sammy," Dad began, "you're growing up. And you're absolutely right. Things change. Right now you are missing being a little kid with no troubles, no jobs to do, and no grades to get. When you were a little kid, Mommy and Daddy always defended you and made sure everything was fair. Now that you're getting bigger, there's a lot you have to do for yourself."

"Yeah," Sammy cried, "and I hate it. This is going to be terrible. It's terrible now!"

"Well," replied Dad, "it's all in how you look at it."

"What does that mean?" asked Sammy.

"Let's look at everything that's happened in the last few days. I'll bet that you can find a new way to look at each and every thing that happened in a way that makes you love your life."

"I don't see how, Daddy," said Sammy.

Dad said, "Well, let's look at the art you do. Mommy, Daddy, Grandma, and Gramps love everything that you do because it's from you. We all love you and are happy that you love to draw. Miss Caroline likes you and she knows that you are capable of doing even better art. She just wants to help you make that happen.

"Peter is your best friend," Dad went on. "He will always be your good friend no matter how many other new people you both meet. Next time why don't you invite Peter *and* Kenny to come over and play?"

Sammy nodded his head. "Daddy, I think I get it. I was looking at everything as bad. You made those things look like they could also be good. Let me try now.

"When I take the trash out it's like having a job. You work to earn money for us to buy stuff. I work so I can do my fun stuff."

"Exactly right!" replied Dad.

"I don't know how to make Grandma and the paint better," said Sammy.

"Well, Sammy, Grandma loves you and isn't really angry at you. She just wants you to think before you do things. When you stop and think about whether or not something is a good thing to do, you can sometimes make sure problems don't happen. If you're not sure, ask Mommy or me, Gramps, Grandma, Miss Caroline, or a friend's parents if they think it's okay."

"I don't know, Daddy. It seems like a lot to remember."

Dad smiled at Sammy. "Well, son, you're going to be growing up for a long time. That gives you plenty of time to learn all of this!"

"Daddy, I don't really hate my life," said Sammy. "I just hated the last few days. And it felt like they would last forever. Growing up is hard."

"Sometimes it is, son," Dad said lovingly, "but growing up for me meant being able to marry your wonderful mother and have you as my wonderful son. That's not so bad, is it?"

"No," said Sammy with a big grin. "I love you, Daddy."

"I love you too, Sammy. Now let's go home to Mommy."